T0145287

Anxiety isn't me

by
CANDACE CURRY

To order additional copies of this book, contact:
Xlibris
844-714-8691
www.Xlibris.com
Orders@Xlibris.com

ISBN:	Softcover	978-1-6698-2000-0
	EBook	978-1-6698-1999-8

Print information available on the last page

Rev. date: 04/13/2022

For Ciera, the little girl
with SUPER POWERS!

Mommy loves you to the moon
and back, forever and always.
Keep on being SUPER.

- CC

So.... I have ADHD.

Did you know that many kids like me who have ADHD also have anxiety?

is there anyone
like me?"

What that means is that sometimes....

like today,

I feel a little nervous...

I feel a little scared...

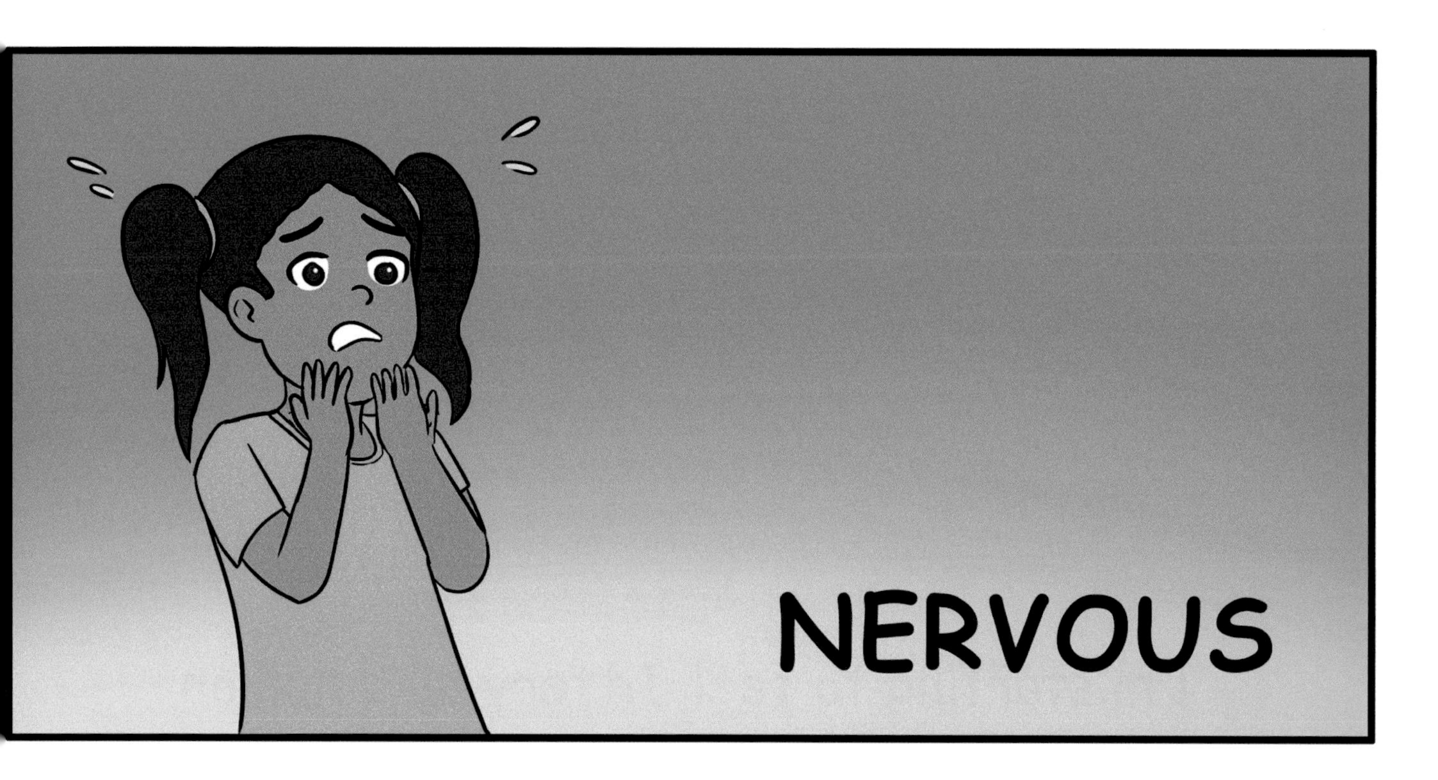
NERVOUS

SCARED

I'm starting to feel Jittery as a million thoughts run through my head.

My mind starts to play the What if game.

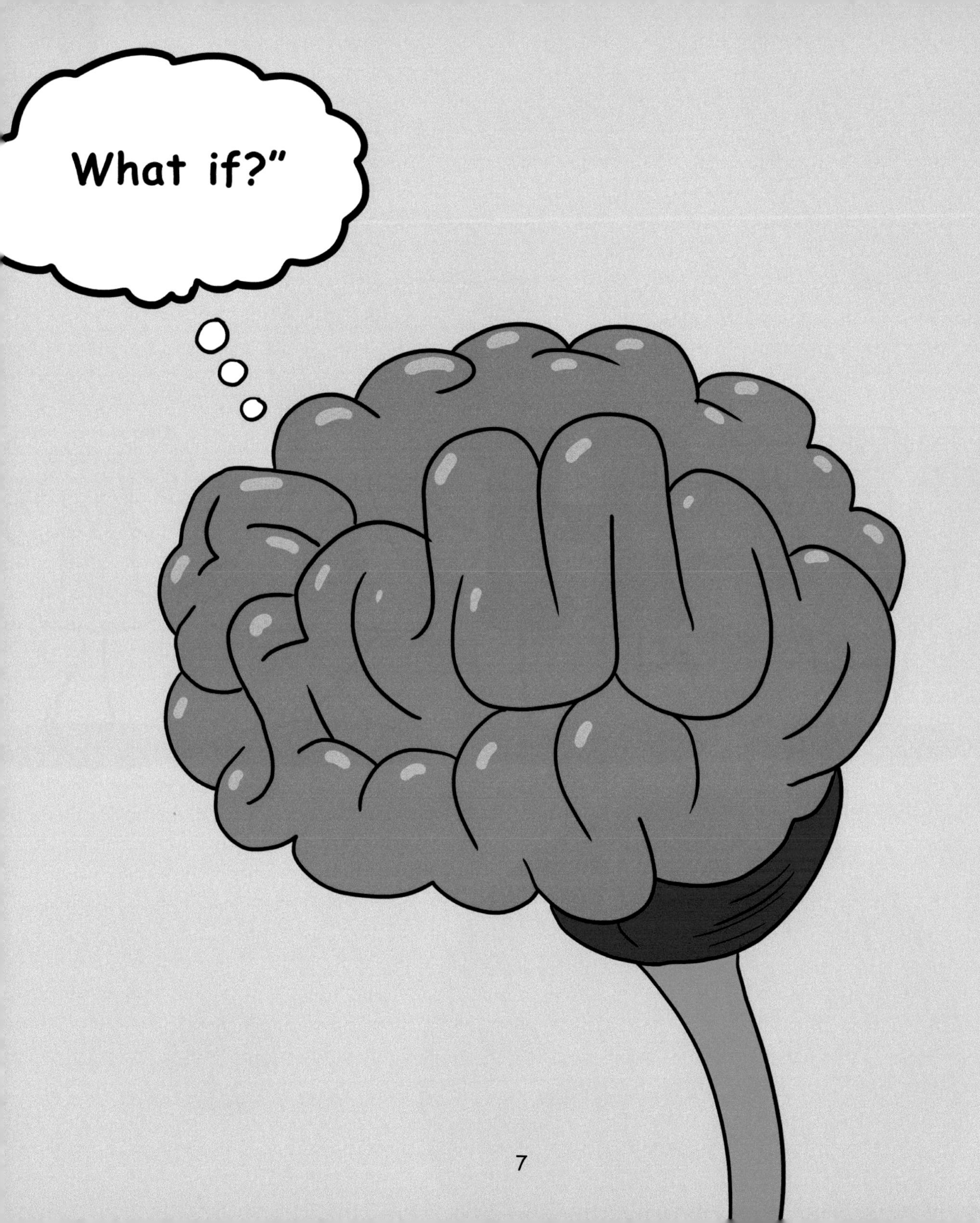
What if?"

What if I get hurt?

What if I get lost?

The what if's
continue and

dance all around

Suddenly my smiles turn to a frown.

I feel the tears start to fill my eyes

This is no surprise as my anxiety starts to rise.

A
N
X
I
E
T
Y

I start to try to think happy thoughts but...

the anxious thoughts are battling
the happy ones- who will win?

Mommy tells me to take deep breaths
in like I'm smelling a rose...

and blow out like I'm blowing a
candle out on a cake...

Wait it starts to work...
I'm feeling better.

I can't wait to tell Mommy that I felt better on my own today.
What do you think she'll say?

ADHD and Anxiety Facts

- **ADHD** stands for Attention- Deficit Hyperactivity Disorder.
- **ADHD and Anxiety**_are often a package deal.
- Sometimes, anxiety comes as a result of ADHD. When that's the case, your worries are often about how much -- or how little -- you're able to get done. You're anxious about or overwhelmed as a result of your your ADHD.
- Millions of children and adults have both ADHD and anxiety.

- Learning focusing techniques to cope with your ADHD often decreases the feeling of anxiety.
- Some people with ADHD are "day dreamers" while others are "overly active or hyper."
- ADHD effects executive functions or the ability to successfully execute or complete tasks.
- ADHD isn't caused by laziness or a lack of discipline.
- ADHD can be a strength. Many people who have been diagnosed with ADHD are highly creative and "outside of the box" thinkers.

About the Author:

The author of this book is my real life Mommy, her name is Candace Curry. She always makes me feel **SUPER!** As a matter of fact she wrote this book just for me as well as **ADHD ISN'T ME!**

Candace Curry, was born and raised in Brooklyn New York where she continues to reside with her family. She is a mother, a Teacher, an entrepreneur and the wearer of many, many hats but the one that she cherishes most is that of mother to her two young daughters.

Printed in the United States
by Baker & Taylor Publisher Services